NICHOLAS · PIPE

Robert D. San Souci
pictures by David Shannon

Dial Books for Young Readers  New York

For Dan & Loretta, Yvette, Justin, & Noelle
with affection as boundless as Nicholas Pipe's ocean
R.D.S.S.

For Heidi, Traci, and Sandra
D.S.

Published by Dial Books for Young Readers
A Division of Penguin Books USA Inc.
375 Hudson Street, New York, New York 10014
Text copyright © 1997 by Robert D. San Souci
Pictures copyright © 1997 by David Shannon
Designed by Atha Tehon
Printed in Hong Kong
First Edition
1 3 5 7 9 10 8 6 4 2

Library of Congress Cataloging in Publication Data
San Souci, Robert D.
Nicholas Pipe / by Robert D. San Souci; pictures by David Shannon.—1st ed.
p.   cm.
Summary: A retelling of a twelfth-century tale in which a young woman falls in love
with a merman and determines to marry him despite their separate worlds.
ISBN 0-8037-1764-4 — ISBN 0-8037-1765-2
[1. Mermen—Folklore.   2. Folklore.]   I. Shannon, David, date, ill.   II. Title.
PZ8.1. S227Ni 1997   398.2—dc20—dc20   [E]   [398.21]   96-8541   CIP   AC

The artwork was rendered in acrylics.

This story is based on a brief account, "Of Nicholas Pipe, a Merman," in Walter Map's *De Nugis Curialium (Courtiers' Trifles)*. Map (c. 1140-1208), an English priest who was a witty storyteller and a noted figure at the court of Henry II, collected these stories, sermons, and bits of folklore and history between 1181 and 1193. While Map's account ends with the merman left for dead by the side of the road, I suggest that he may not have known the full story. For this retelling I consulted the volume translated and edited by Frederick Tupper and Marbury Bladen (New York: The Macmillan Company, 1924).   R.D.S.S.

Long ago, in a seaside village, a young woman named Margaret lived with her father, a fisherman named Marius. She was quick-witted and pretty and wooed by all the young men. But she cared only for handsome Nicholas Pipe.

Nicholas was a merman. Beneath the waves he would swim for hours with his powerful fishtail, but when he left the sea, he walked on two legs like any other man. Sometimes when she was in a boat helping her father haul in his nets, Margaret glimpsed Nicholas racing dolphin-swift through the green depths. Then her heart nearly broke for love of him.

Nicholas chose for an unknown reason to make his home on land, living in a driftwood hut. He did odd jobs for the villagers—mending pots or pushcarts, thatching roofs, helping the fishermen clean and salt their catches. To his neighbors he seemed unremarkable—except when he warned them of coming storms. But to Margaret he was a marvel beyond all others. Still, she dared not speak to him, because her father forbade her.

"Your only brother was drowned when you were an infant," the old man often said bitterly. "Those who brought back his boat said that he was pulled into the sea by merfolk. You must have nothing to do with the likes of Nicholas Pipe."

"Yet he seems so gentle," Margaret would protest.

"Never so much as say 'Good morrow' to him," Marius insisted. And dutiful Margaret sadly agreed.

One morning, after many days of poor catches, Marius rowed far out to a spot known only to himself and his daughter. There the fish were always plentiful.

As Margaret mended nets at home, she was startled to see a friend running down the path. "Nicholas Pipe says a storm is coming!" he cried. "Tell your father to tie up his boats!"

Margaret hurried to the shore and launched the boat that had been her brother's. She saw her neighbors waving her back, and glimpsed Nicholas Pipe in their midst. But she put her sturdy back into her rowing, and soon she was far from land.

The sky darkened; the breeze turned to gusting wind; the waves grew higher. Margaret forced her aching arms to work the oars even more urgently.

At last she spotted her father. "A storm is coming!" she shouted. "We must return at once!"

"Help me draw in the nets," Marius called back.

Margaret came alongside. Together they hauled up the nets, spilling the fish into both boats.

The sky turned black, and rain mixed with the freezing wind. The boats pitched and rolled as Margaret tied her craft behind and climbed into her father's boat. Each took an oar and rowed desperately.

From the gathering dark and churning waves came screeches and the murmur of voices speaking a strange language.

"We are doomed!" groaned Marius. "Those are the sea-folk." Margaret saw pale shapes flash beneath her dipping oar.

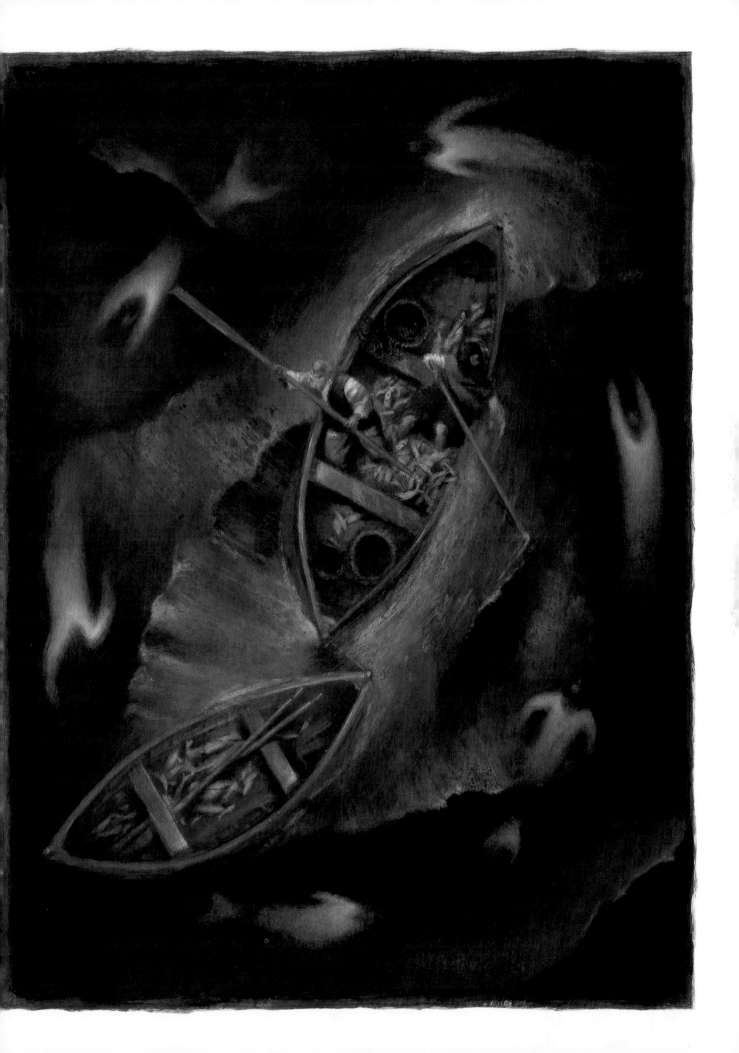

Then Margaret heard her name called as two arms reached over the gunwale. Marius lunged to pull his daughter away; but he slipped and fell, knocking himself senseless.

"Father!" shouted Margaret. At that moment a figure hoisted itself into the boat. Margaret gave an astonished cry: "Nicholas Pipe!"

Nicholas put a finger to his lips, and she was silent. Cradling her father's head, Margaret watched Nicholas lean out and whisper to the waves.

He was answered by growls and shrieks. Pale shapes leaped from the water. Eyes as black and soulless as a shark's glared at Margaret. Then the sea-folk vanished with angry splashes.

As the sounds faded and the water grew calmer, Nicholas took Marius's oar. "Row for your life!" he urged Margaret. "The charm I spoke will only keep my sisters away for a short time."

"You were kind to rescue us," Margaret said. "My father is no friend to you."

Nicholas looked away. "I try to keep all village folk safe from the sea and storms. It is how I make return for your letting me live among you."

The harbor came into view. As Nicholas and Margaret brought the boats to shore, Marius sat up, rubbing his head. Seeing Nicholas, he shook his fist, shouting, "Begone, you wicked creature!"

With a glance at Margaret, the merman hurried up the beach.

"For shame, Father," Margaret said. "He saved us."

"His kind drowned your brother," answered the old man. "Promise me that you will never speak to him again."

"I cannot do that," she said defiantly.

"He has turned you against me," Marius responded. "Heaven help him for that!"

So they returned to their cottage, wet and wretched and wrapped in thoughts as gloomy as the day.

The next morning Marius announced he was leaving on a long journey.

"Where are you going?" asked Margaret in surprise.

"That is my affair," her father said peevishly. Soon after this he set out. "Stay away from Nicholas Pipe," he warned.

"You misjudge him, Father," Margaret said sadly.

From the window she watched the old man until he was hidden by a turn in the path that wound over the nearby hills. Suddenly she spotted Nicholas walking toward the shore.

She ran to him, calling, "Nicholas Pipe! I never thanked you for helping my father and myself."

"Well, now you have done so." He continued on his way.

"Please stay," she begged. "You need not fear my father. He has gone away, and I do not know when he will return."

"I am sorry he dislikes me," Nicholas said. "But I am not afraid of him."

Margaret's fingers brushed his arm, and he trembled. "Is it I who frightens you?" she asked softly.

He did not answer her directly, but said, "I come from the sea, a place of wonder and beauty—but also filled with danger and cruelty. I grew weary of it, and longed to visit your world beyond the reach of the waves.

"One day I saved a child from drowning. In thanks, her father, a sorcerer, cast the spell that lets me live among land-folk. But I must touch the sea every day, or I will die."

"You still have not told me what I have done to distress you," said Margaret.

"I live halfway between land and sea," sighed Nicholas. "Yet when I see you, I long to be fully a part of your world."

Margaret's heart was flooded with joy. "Why, Nicholas Pipe," she said gently, "you sound very much like a man in love."

"Yes," he said miserably.

"And I feel the same about you. Ask me to be your wife," she said, "and when my father returns, I will make him give us his blessing."

Nicholas shook his head. "I am a child of the sea. You are a child of this world. We can never wed. It would be better if I went away."

"No!" she exclaimed. "Stay: I could not bear to think that I had driven you away."

He smiled sadly. "I will stay then. But do not speak to me, and I will not speak to you. It breaks my heart."

At this Nicholas plunged into the waves and vanished.

A few days later, as Margaret set off for an errand in town, she heard shouts from the village square. Hurrying her steps, she came upon a horrifying sight: Nicholas Pipe was imprisoned in a cage set upon a cart. The king's horsemen kept the villagers back.

"Nicholas!" Margaret shouted. She pushed through the crowd, but was blocked by soldiers.

"What has he done?" Margaret asked.

"He is a merman," the commander said. "The king collects

strange things. He ordered us to bring this marvel to him."

"He will die if he is kept from the sea!" she cried.

"I obey the king," replied the commander. "Stand aside!"

Margaret grabbed his arm as if to unhorse him. He raised his sword, but someone shouted, "Spare my daughter!"

Margaret saw her father clamber from his seat beside the cart driver. He pulled her away as the cart and horsemen thundered down the road that led inland across the hills.

Margaret tried to follow, but Marius held her back.

"*You* went to the king," Margaret accused her father. "You betrayed Nicholas to him!"

"It is for the best," he said, unable to look at her.

"No, Father. It is bad for all the village because Nicholas can no longer warn us when storms are due. It is worse for me, because I love him. And it is worst for poor, blameless Nicholas, because he will die if he cannot touch the sea."

Margaret ran and fetched two waterskins from her cottage. Wading into the sea, she filled them with saltwater. As her father buried his head in his hands, she headed for the road that the soldiers and their prisoner had taken.

When night fell, Margaret let the moon and stars light her path. Early the next morning she came upon the king's men, arguing beneath a tree. Nicholas lay propped against the trunk.

"Is he ill?" Margaret asked, kneeling beside him.

"He is dead," said one soldier.

"The king will have our heads," said another.

"Leave him," their commander decided. "We will tell the king that he escaped into the sea."

So they rode off, leaving Margaret beside the merman.

"Oh, my poor Nicholas," she said, weeping. Her salt tears rained down on his face.

His eyelids fluttered. Then he opened his eyes and looked into hers. "You have brought the life-giving sea to me," he whispered. "The touch of it is in your tears."

"I have done better!" she cried joyfully. Swiftly she took one waterskin and poured brine over him. Strength returned to his limbs. With her help he was able to stand.

They began the journey back along the dusty road. When he weakened, he doused himself with saltwater. But the first waterskin was soon empty. As the day grew hotter, Nicholas needed more and more water to keep up his strength.

With the second waterskin nearly drained, Margaret fearfully watched the sun climb higher into the sky.

On they struggled toward the sea. But Nicholas grew weaker; Margaret could squeeze only a drop or two from the waterskins.

Then, as they reached the foot of the hills, Margaret spotted her father approaching. To her surprise, Marius put his arm around Nicholas's shoulders, helping support him.

"Why are you doing this?" Margaret asked as they half carried, half dragged a fainting Nicholas between them.

"Because I love my daughter who loves him so much," Marius explained. "And because our neighbors blame me for taking him from the village. I have sinned against them, against you, and against Nicholas, who saved both our lives."

When the waterskins were empty, Marius sliced them open. Margaret pressed the damp insides to Nicholas's forehead. This kept him strong enough to reach the crest of the hill.

With a prayer of thanks, they saw below them the village and the blue shining sea. A salt-breeze from the shore revived all three. Together they raced toward the water.

People shouted excitedly, "Nicholas Pipe has come back!" as Margaret, Nicholas, and Marius tumbled gratefully into the cool waves. Nicholas swam away, dove, rose, waved, and dove again. Then there was no trace of him.

"Forgive me," said Marius. Father and daughter stood ankle-deep in the water, watching the empty sea.

"I do," said Margaret. "And I am sure Nicholas forgives you too. But I tell you, if he has not gone away, and if he will have me, I will become his wife."

"I confess the thought still makes me uneasy," said Marius, "but I will give you both my blessing."

"Look!" cried Margaret. "There is Nicholas!"

Indeed, the merman was wading across the shallows toward her. With a splash, he dropped to his knees before her. Then he placed a perfect pearl in her palm. "This is only one of the treasures I will bring you," he said, "if you will be my bride."

"Your love is treasure enough, Nicholas Pipe," she replied.

"It will not be easy," he said. "I am a child of the sea; you are a child of the land."

"Yes," she said. "But our children will be children of land and sea, and Oh! what marvels they will be."